ONE DAY IN A'NH'S WORLD

I am A'nh. I live in Quang Ngai Province,
Vietnam with my mum and dad.
They are called 'Ma' and 'Bo' here.
Grandma – 'Ba Noi' - lives with us too.

4

Our village is on
the Trà Khúc River,
which opens to the
South China Sea.

I play by the river,
while other people fish
and wash clothes
in the water.

5

Inside our hut I play with my dolls. Outside I help Ba Noi look after our pig and ducks.

6

Ba Noi and I share a rice congee 'Chao'
with vegetables for lunch.
Vietnamese broccoli is my favourite.

After lunch, Ba Noi helps me unroll
my sleeping mat for a rest in our hut.
She may have an afternoon nap too.

After a rest, Ba Noi takes me to the market to buy watermelon and papaya. Ba Noi's old friend has a stall selling spices. They talk about the heat. For shade, we are wearing our 'Non La' – Vietnamese hats.

9

Occasionally, Ba Noi and I will journey to the Ba To Garden.
She likes to sit and think there.
I look at the colourful flowers and birds.

Ma and Bo work in the rice paddies, then return home for dinner. We eat rice with a fish sauce, but we don't eat too much of the crop so that we still have some to sell. Sometimes we have duck eggs as a treat.

Ma and Bo will have time off to celebrate New Year. Last time they had a rest from the fields was for Buddha's Birthday – 'Vesak' - and we celebrated and shared food with other people in the village.

Before bed, I check on the chickens behind our hut with Ba Noi.

ONE DAY IN KWASI'S WORLD

I am Kwasi. I live on the Marsibit plains in Kenya with my mother 'Haadha', two older brothers and an aunt, two uncles and four cousins.

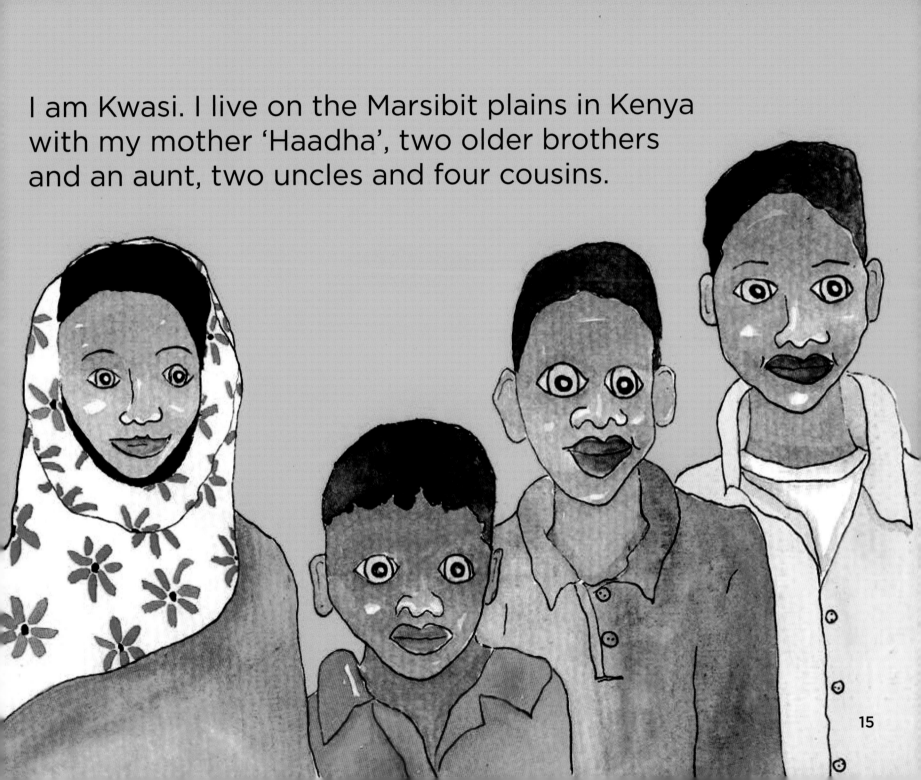

We are nomadic people, my home is the desert.
My brothers look after our camel herd.
Sometimes I follow them.

When we set up camp I go with Haadha to the closest watering hole to collect our supply of water for the day.

During the day I have milk with maize
which is porridge called 'posho'.

I rest in the shade with Haadha under a
desert acacia. Haadha shields me with a
cool sheet. The sun is hot, it makes us tired.

19

In the afternoon Haadha takes me into
Marsabit town to collect bananas.
She has a hot tea drink with her sister
who lives in the town. I play out the front
with a ball while I wait for her.

20

Sometimes I go to Lake Paradise with my brothers.
We see elephants and water buffalo swimming in the water.

At night we all sit together around the campfire and eat Banana porridge. My older brother amuses us, he is a good storyteller.

We also talk about the Eid-ul-Adha festival that has just past.
My family celebrated by eating goat and camel meats.
We are Gabbra people, a group from the Borana tribe.
A long time ago we practiced our native religion Waaqa,
but today we are Muslims.

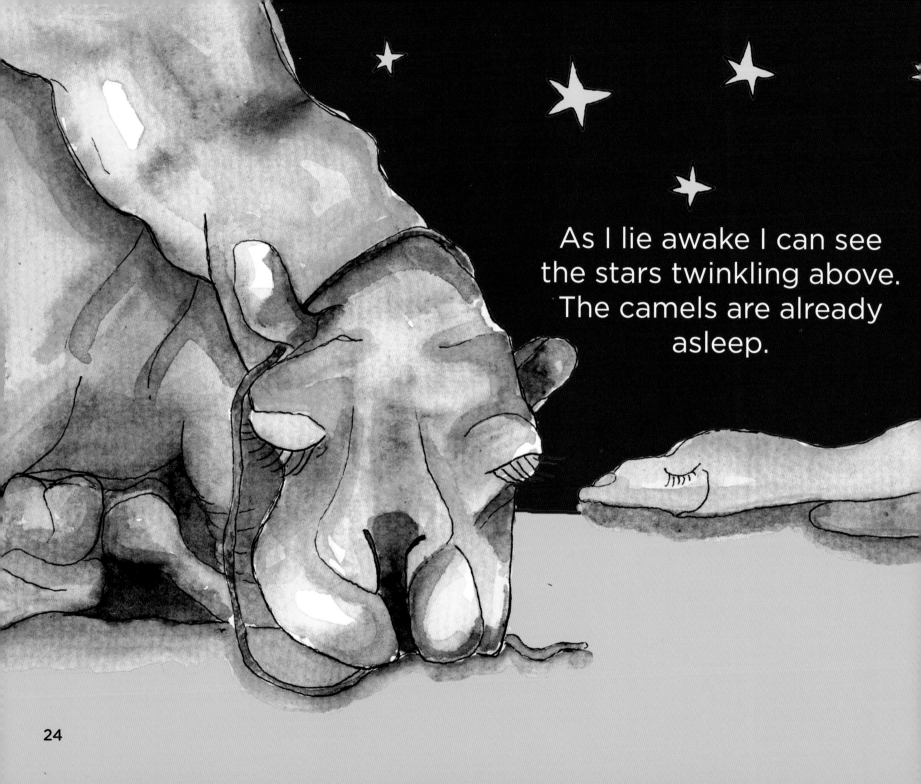

As I lie awake I can see the stars twinkling above. The camels are already asleep.

24

ONE DAY IN JOSHUA'S WORLD

I am Joshua. I live in a suburb of Melbourne, Australia with Mum and Dad.

Our home is near the park. I go there to play.
Gum trees surround the park and a creek flows through it
from the nearby lake.

The ducks waddle on
the grass and the native
rosellas fly overhead.

27

Back at home I play with my toy aeroplane and cars.
I watch my favourite shows on the TV.
I help Mum unpack the dishwasher.

Mum gives me a delicious chicken sandwich for lunch and some fruit and blueberry yoghurt too.

After lunch, I have a sleep in my bed.
My teddies watch me from the shelf.
I dream as music plays.

Later, Mum takes me to the shopping centre.
We meet friends and Mum has a chat and coffee with them.
I have a strawberry milk shake. I help Mum carry
the groceries for our dinner. They feel heavier
the longer Mum looks in the ladies dress shop!

31

As a special treat, Mum sometimes likes to take me to the Zoo.
We see the lions roar and the gorillas parade in their enclosure.
The giraffe's long neck is incredible.

32

Dad has returned from the office by train just in time for dinner. We eat my favourite spaghetti and meatballs, with peaches and ice cream to follow – mmm yum!

Mum and Dad talk about plans for Christmas, who will come for lunch and presents to buy. I will help decorate the freshly cut pine tree with tinsel, ornaments and colourful lights. We are Christians and celebrate Christmas, to recognise the birth of baby Jesus long ago.

After dinner, I play with my best friend Henry, our dog, before bed.

This is **our** World.

We are all special and unique.
We hope for happiness for each other.

Published by Brolga Publishing Pty Ltd
ABN 46 063 962 443
PO Box 12544
A'Beckett St
Melbourne, VIC, 8006
Australia

email: markzocchi@brolgapublishing.com.au

National Library of Australia Cataloguing-in-Publication entry

Author: Sara Mithen
Illustrator: Natalie Stone
Title: One day in our world
ISBN: 9781922175311 (hardback)
Target Audience: For children.
Subjects: Children--Australia--Social life and customs--Juvenile fiction.
           Children--Australia--Social conditions--Juvenile fiction.
           Children--Vietnam--Social life and customs--Juvenile fiction.
           Children--Vietnam--Social conditions--Juvenile fiction.
           Children--Kenya--Social life and customs--Juvenile fiction.
           Children--Kenya--Social conditions--Juvenile fiction.

Dewey Number: A823.4

Printed in China
Illustrations by Natalie Stone
Typesetting by Wanissa Somsuphangsri

BE PUBLISHED

Publish through a successful publisher.
Brolga Publishing is represented through:

• National book trade distribution, including sales, marketing & distribution through Macmillan Australia.
• International book trade distribution to
    • The United Kingdom
    • North America
    • Sales representation in South East Asia
• Worldwide e-Book distribution

For details and inquiries, contact:
Brolga Publishing Pty Ltd
PO Box 12544
A'Beckett St VIC 8006

Phone: 0414 608 494
markzocchi@brolgapublishing.com.au
ABN: 46 063 962 443
(Email for a catalogue request)